CATHY KELLY

LETTER FROM CHICAGO

Cathy Kelly is the author of five novels: *What She Wants*, *Someone Like You*, *Never Too Late*, *She's The One* and *Woman To Woman*, all Number One bestsellers. She lives with her partner in County Wicklow.

NEW ISLAND *Open Door*

LETTER FROM CHICAGO
First published January 2002
by New Island
2 Brookside
Dundrum Road
Dublin 14

www.newisland.ie

A CIP catalogue record for this book is available from the British Library

ISBN -10: 1 902602 69 2
ISBN -13: 978 1 902602 69 1

New Island Books receives financial assistance from
The Arts Council (An Chomhairle Ealaíon), Dublin,
Ireland.

arts
council
chomhairle
ealaíon

Typeset by New Island
Printed in Great Britain by CPD (Wales) Ltd, Ebbw Vale.
Cover design by Artmark

3 5 4 2

NEW ISLAND *Open Door*

Welcome to the third Open Door series. Once again, some of Ireland's best-loved authors have come up with a wonderful array of books for this unique series. Branching out for the first time into non-fiction, Tom Nestor's warm and moving childhood memoir will ring bells with many who grew up in 1940s' rural Ireland, while Margaret Neylon introduces us to the secret of numbers, or 'numerology', and invites us to have a look at what's in store in our lives. Add to this four diverse stories from best-selling authors Maeve Binchy, Vincent Banville, Cathy Kelly and Deirdre Purcell — from family feud and the bloom of late romance, to crime-solving on Dublin's mean streets and unravelling secrets and lies inside a family home — and you will find something here to suit everyone's taste. And, like all good stories, we hope these books will open doors — of the imagination and of opportunity — for adult readers of all ages.

All royalties from the Irish sales of the Open Door series go to a charity of the author's choice. *Letter From Chicago* royalties go to the Alzheimer Society of Ireland.

.

THE OPEN DOOR SERIES IS DEVELOPED WITH THE ASSISTANCE OF THE CITY OF DUBLIN VOCATIONAL EDUCATION COMMITTEE.

Dear Reader,

On behalf of myself and the other contributing authors, I would like to welcome you to the third Open Door series. We hope that you enjoy the novels and that reading becomes a lasting pleasure in your life.

Warmest wishes,

Patricia Scanlan.

Patricia Scanlan
Series Editor

To Mum
With love

Chapter One

Elsie loved letters from Chicago. She adored the fat envelopes with their colourful American stamps. Even the postmarks looked exotic and exciting.

On the first Monday in March, the postman arrived early with a letter from Chicago. As usual, Elsie was the first person up in the McDonnell house. She was making a cup of tea in the kitchen when she heard the postman.

She put down the milk carton and went slowly into the hall to collect the post. Elsie went everywhere slowly. She was sixty-five and had arthritis. Sometimes, every part of her body ached. This morning, only her hands were sore. It had taken her ages to turn on the tap to fill the kettle. Tom, her son-in-law, said he'd get her a special yoke to help her turn the tap on. But Elsie had said no. She wasn't an invalid. She didn't want to be treated like one.

There was only one letter on the mat in the hall and it was for her.

Smiling, she went back into the kitchen. She sat at the kitchen table to read her letter. From upstairs, she could hear the Monday morning sounds of everyone else getting up.

Kim was begging the twins to get out of bed.

'I won't let you watch television on Sunday nights if you can't get up for school next morning,' she warned.

She said the same thing every Monday morning. She was too soft on those girls, Elsie thought.

But then, Kim was soft on everyone. Elsie had no idea how Kim managed to keep a class of eight-year-olds under control in St Mary's Primary School.

Elsie heard Tom stomping into the bathroom. He was a big man and made as much noise as an elephant.

Next, the twins turned their CD player on. Loud music could be heard all over the house.

'Turn that music down!' roared Tom. 'I have a headache!'

Emer roared back that it wasn't loud at all. Didn't he like The Corrs?

Satisfied that everything was normal in the McDonnell house, Elsie began to read the letter from her sister in Chicago. Maisie had gone to America forty-five years before. But she wrote home every month. They talked about their families in the letters. Elsie loved hearing about Maisie's two children and her four grandchildren. In turn, she wrote happily about her three children. She had six grandchildren, two more than Maisie. Elsie was pleased about that.

Dear Elsie,

I have the most amazing news for you. Charleen is going to visit you in Ireland in the last week of August. Isn't that exciting? She wants to meet all the family. I can't tell you how happy I am that my granddaughter is going to visit Dublin.

I told Charleen she'd be welcome to stay with you. Her friend is going with her as they are only eighteen. I hope I did the right thing …

Elsie stopped reading and took a

shaky sip of tea. She was stunned. No, it was worse than that. She was shocked, really shocked. What ever was she going to do?

★

Kim McDonnell was the last person to get into the bathroom. That was the routine. Tom used it first. He left towels on the floor no matter what Kim said. He didn't mean to, she knew that. It was his upbringing. Tom had been born into a house with four older sisters and an adoring mother. When he'd married Kim, he'd never washed up after a meal in his life. He had to be told how to use the washing machine. He still thought you could wash black clothes with white clothes.

The twins used the bathroom after Tom. They left more towels on the floor and forgot to close the shampoo bottle properly. They wasted loads of shampoo that way.

'Ah Mum, don't nag,' they would say when she complained.

They were studying for their exams. As a teacher, Kim knew that it was important not to upset kids before big exams.

'Young people doing exams need to have a calm home life,' said all the experts.

Kim liked a calm home life herself. It wasn't easy to feel calm with two fifteen-year-olds in the house. The exams were in three months and Kim couldn't wait for them to be over. In August, the whole family was going to Brittas to stay in a mobile home for three weeks. Kim thought about relaxing in the sun and not having to go to work. She thought about nice meals on the deck outside the mobile

home and no screaming children to
teach. Roll on August.

She had a quick shower and washed
her long, dark hair. She didn't bother
drying it. Instead, she brushed it neatly
and tied it back with a band. She put
on a bit of lipstick and mascara. Kim
never used much make-up.

Tom said she didn't need it.

'You're lovely as you are,' he'd say,
kissing her.

Tom was an awful liar, Kim thought
with a smile. She wasn't bad looking.
She had big dark eyes, creamy pale skin
and nice hair. But she wasn't Julia
Roberts.

People who looked like Julia Roberts
didn't have to work long hours to pay
the mortgage. They didn't worry about
money or about the children doing well
at school. They went to parties in big
cars and bought expensive clothes.

Kim buttoned up the pink blouse she had bought in Dunnes for twenty-five euro. Still, she was happy.

★

The twins listened to their new Corrs CD and put on their make-up. The head nun didn't like students to wear make-up. But Emer and Laura didn't care.

Emer closed one eye as she put on black eye-liner.

'Mum will kill you if she sees you wearing that much eye-liner,' Laura said. Laura was the sensible twin.

'She won't kill me,' said Emer confidently. She did the other eye. 'Do I look like Britney Spears?' she asked.

'No,' said her sister.

Emer grinned.

'I wish we didn't have a test in Irish today,' Laura said. 'I know I'll fail.'

'It will be easy,' said Emer. She was good at Irish. She didn't understand how Laura wasn't good at it. Twins were supposed to be the same at everything. But then, Laura had no interest in clothes. She didn't get excited by the thoughts of a sale in Top Shop. And she didn't seem that keen on guys either. Not really, anyway. She agreed that David O'Regan in sixth year was handsome. But she'd never dream of chatting him up. Emer smiled at him for all she was worth every morning at assembly.

'Girls, come down for breakfast!' shouted their mother.

Emer sighed. She put on another bit of eye-liner for luck. When she was sixteen, she was going to dye her hair blonde. She was fed up with brown hair. She wanted bright blonde, the sort of hair that women from Sweden had. Boys loved blondes. Emer smiled to herself. Perhaps she wouldn't wait until she was sixteen.

★

Tom McDonnell didn't sit at the kitchen table for breakfast. He ate a piece of toast standing up. He had a job in Rathfarnham at half nine. The traffic would be mad at this time of the morning. His mother-in-law usually gave out to him when he didn't eat a proper breakfast. She said nothing today. He ate his toast and wondered if she was sick.

At ten to eight, he was ready to leave the house.

'Bye, love,' he said to Kim. He kissed her goodbye. 'Bye Elsie, bye girls.'

'Bye Dad,' answered the girls. Elsie didn't speak. She had to be sick, Tom thought. Elsie never stopped talking. She talked about the neighbours, about bingo, and about her sister in America. Elsie had lived with them for two years, since she'd been widowed. Tom had learned not to listen. He liked Elsie but she talked enough for four people.

He shut the front door and thought it could do with a lick of paint. The whole house could do with a lick of paint. There just weren't enough hours in the day, Tom decided as he got into the van. McDonnell's Electrical Services, read the writing on the side. It had been a big step to set up his own business. That was five years ago.

Now, he was always busy. But money was still tight. Every time he looked, the twins needed new clothes or new shoes. Kim's car needed replacing. It would fall apart one of these days. He might buy a lottery ticket with his lunch.

Chapter Two

'What's wrong, Mother?' asked Kim when Tom was gone.

She knew that *something* was wrong with her mother. Elsie's face was white under its dusting of pinky face-powder. She had said no to a second cup of tea. She had stared into space for ages. Even worse, she hadn't given out to the twins about their loud music. Rows about loud music made up most of the arguments in the house. 'Nothing's wrong,' said Elsie. She drained the rest of her cold tea.

'Mother …' warned Kim. 'I'm not blind. Please tell me what's wrong.'

Elsie knew it was time to be honest. 'This came this morning.' She handed the letter to her daughter.

Kim read it carefully. Her face got grimmer with each word. 'Aunt Maisie has a nerve!' she said when she had finished. She was furious. There was no room in their house for two American visitors. There was no room for any visitor. They only had three bedrooms. Where did Aunt Maisie think the Americans would sleep? In the garden? On the roof with next door's ginger cat?

'What's wrong?' asked Laura, her mouth full of cornflakes.

Kim was furious. 'Your Aunt Maisie in Chicago has told us that Charleen is coming to stay. In August and with a friend.'

'Cool!' said Emer. She had never

met her American cousin. She wondered if Charleen would look like a movie star. American teenagers on television all looked like movie stars. They never seemed to have spots and they all had long legs. Emer dreamed about having long, long legs.

'Where will they sleep?' asked Laura. She was the practical one.

'I don't know where they will sleep.' Kim was still angry. 'This is a small house. Why does Aunt Maisie think we have room for two guests?'

Elsie bit her lip.

'I think that's my fault,' Elsie said in a small voice.

The eight o'clock news began on the radio.

'Blast. We're going to be late,' said Kim crossly. She always left before the news.

'Come on, girls, you'll be late too if

you don't get a move on.' Kim quickly shoved the breakfast dishes in the sink. 'I'll do them tonight,' she told her mother. 'And then you can tell me what this is all about.'

The school where she worked was very near the twins' school, so she dropped them off every morning. Emer and Laura always fought about who sat in the back of the car. The Mini was well over twenty years old and the back seat was uncomfortable. This morning, they didn't discuss where they'd sit. They knew that their normally easy-going mother was in a rare temper. Laura hopped quietly in the back.

'I bet your grandmother has been inviting Maisie to stay with us for years, without telling me!' Kim raged. 'I don't want Maisie turning up here. I've never met her in my life! We can do without rich relatives landing here.'

The twins said nothing.

Laura wondered what it must be like for Gran to have a sister she hadn't seen for over forty years. Gran had told her about growing up in the farm in Leitrim. She and Maisie had been the youngest in a big family. There was a year between them, so they were like twins.

'I remember spending hours getting ready to go to dances,' Gran had fondly recalled. 'Maisie would try and sneak out of the house without Da seeing that she was wearing red lipstick,' Gran said. Maisie had a great romance with a local lad around about the time Gran had met Grandad. But the lad Maisie liked was the oldest son and he was getting the farm.

'Maisie wasn't one for settling down on another farm. She couldn't wait to get out of the West,' Gran said sadly.

'She had her heart set on America for years. This lad came home from Boston to his mother's funeral and Maisie upped and married him.'

'Why did she never come back to visit, Gran?' Laura asked.

Gran shrugged. 'It wasn't like now, Laura,' she said. 'Plane journeys were expensive. Maisie lived in Oregon for a long time. That's a long way away. She always meant to come home but it never happened. And then, her children were growing up.' Elsie didn't tell Laura that she'd often wondered herself why Maisie hadn't wanted to come back to Ireland. They'd shared so much as children. It hurt that her sister could stay away for so long. Elsie and her husband, Ted, God rest him, had never been rich. They couldn't afford to fly to America. But sure, wasn't Maisie as rich as sin? She could have afforded to fly home. And her two children had great jobs as a doctor and a dentist. They could have given her money too. Elsie could never understand why Maisie had stayed away so long.

Sitting in the back of the car, Laura looked at her twin sister. Emer was tapping her fingers along to the song on the radio. Sometimes, Emer drove her mad. But Laura would hate to spend forty-something years without seeing her.

★

Class 3A were quiet as mice all day. This was not normal. But sweet Mrs McDonnell looked so angry that they were all scared of making noise. Even Barry Smith was good and he was always the boldest boy in the whole school.

Barry had a water pistol in his

pocket. He'd planned to fire it at everyone when the teacher wasn't looking. Then he saw the cross look on Mrs McDonnell's face. He hoped she wasn't angry with him. She was never angry. But just in case, he put the water pistol back in his school bag. There was always tomorrow.

At the top of the class, Kim McDonnell tried to concentrate. It wasn't that she didn't want to see poor Charleen. They'd love to see her. But where could she sleep? And why did Aunt Maisie think they had loads of room?

23 St Jude's Villas was not a big house. Not like her brother Rob's house. He lived in a detached house in Raheny. He had a spare bedroom for guests.

Kim's house didn't even have a spare seat for guests. The kitchen was so small that there wasn't room for a dishwasher. Kim would have killed for a dishwasher. She sighed. Whatever her mother had said, it was all a big mess.

★

Emer and Laura sat beside each other in school. Between classes, they talked with their friends.

'I bet she's got blonde hair,' Emer said dreamily.

'Who?' asked Laura.

'Charleen. Will she bring presents, do you think? I'd love real American jeans, not ones like you get here.'

'The ones you get here *are* American, stupid,' said Laura.

The Irish teacher marched into the classroom. Laura felt sick. She hated Irish and she hated exams.

'Will you help me if I get stuck on any questions?' she whispered to her twin.

But Emer wasn't listening. She was

20

in dreamland, thinking of the American visit.

★

Elsie was off her food. She had a cup of tea with Mary across the street but didn't fancy one of her friend's scones.

Mary was talking too much to notice. Mary's eldest grandson was in trouble at school for vandalism. He might be thrown out, Mary said. She suffered with those children, Elsie thought. Mary's troubles made her feel guilty. After all, there were no real problems in Kim's house. The twins were good girls, for all their loud music. They wouldn't dream of vandalising anything at school. Their father would kill them. Tom might be a man of few words, but he wouldn't stand any nonsense from the girls.

After tea with Mary, Elsie walked to the chemist for her tablets. The chemist always chatted to her. Today, Elsie didn't chat back.

'Are you not feeling yourself, Elsie?' he asked.

Elsie said she was fine and tried to smile. There was no way out of it. She had to tell Kim the truth.

★

When Kim got home that afternoon, there was a great smell of cooking in the house. Things must be really bad, she thought. Elsie never cooked any more. She baked cakes and her lemon sponge was admired at local church sales. But she didn't cook dinners.

'I made a chicken casserole,' said Elsie brightly when Kim went into the kitchen.

She looked up from peeling potatoes and saw Kim's pale, angry face. Kim was a good daughter. She had a lot on her plate, what with teaching those youngsters in school. Elsie felt her heart become heavy with guilt. She left the potatoes in the sink.

'Sit down,' said Elsie. 'I'll tell you. It's all my fault. I lied to Maisie.'

She looked so miserable that Kim felt sorry she'd been so cross. She patted her mother's hand. 'Go on,' she said.

Elsie sighed. 'You know that Maisie's eldest is a doctor and that Sandra, Charleen's mother, is a dentist.'

Kim nodded. She knew all this. When she'd been growing up, she got fed up hearing about her clever cousins, the Madison family from Chicago. Aunt Maisie's letters had been full of praise for her children. Cousin Sandra was the prettiest girl in her school and was so clever. The teachers had never seen anyone so bright. And popular, Aunt Maisie always added. Phil was the best in the school at maths. He was good at baseball too.

Kim had hated the sound of her goody-two-shoes cousins. They sounded awful. She hoped she never had to meet them. And she never did. She'd never met her Aunt Maisie, for that matter. The Madisons had never come home from America to visit. They hadn't even come for Kim's dad's funeral two years ago. Elsie had been very upset at that, Kim knew. But she'd never said anything.

'You're going to be so mad at me,' said Elsie miserably, thinking of the letter.

'I won't, Mother,' replied Kim. 'Tell me the story, will you?'

'Maisie was a great one for boasting when we were children,' Elsie began.

'She always had to have the nicest dress or the best toy. She loved to show people that she had the best of everything. When she told me how well they were all doing in Chicago, I got fed up. I told her all about you and your sister but ...' Elsie looked really miserable now. 'I lied. I told her that you were the principal of the school.'

Kim gasped.

Elsie ploughed on. 'I told her Tom is the boss of a big company and that you live in a huge house in a posh estate on the outskirts of the county.'

Kim gasped some more.

'And that the girls had ponies and you had a housekeeper.'

'Mother!' said Kim finally. 'How could you make-up all that stuff?'

'I never thought she'd find out,' protested Elsie. 'She was always going on about her pair and how successful they were. Sandra has a housekeeper, so I said you did too.'

'And now Sandra's daughter is coming here. And she thinks we have a big house and a housekeeper,' Kim said. She looked around the kitchen. The wood-effect lino on the floor was ten years old. The kitchen units were orange. Orange had been big in the Seventies when the house was built. Kim hated orange but kitchen units cost a fortune. There had been no money to spend on the house for ages. Setting up Tom's business had been tough. The twins had wanted to go on that school trip to France and Kim hadn't wanted to say no. Clothes for teenagers cost a fortune. The kitchen had been last on the list.

'What are we going to do?' wailed Elsie.

'You'll have to tell Maisie the truth,'

Kim said finally. 'We don't mind Charleen and her friend staying here. But they'll have to sleep in sleeping bags. We can turn the dining room into a room for them. I'll push the table back but that's it.'

Elsie looked as if she could cry.

'What else can I do, Mother?' asked Kim. She felt like crying herself.

Chapter Three

Miles away, Clodagh Dunne sat at her big desk in a city-centre office. She stared through the glass doors in front of her. Clodagh was Kim's younger sister and Elsie's youngest child. In her letters to Chicago, Elsie always said Clodagh worked in Ireland's top advertising company. Elsie made it sound as if Clodagh ran the company. In a way, she did. She was the receptionist and took all the phone calls. The boss joked that the company would fall apart if Clodagh didn't keep them all on their toes. She was very good at her job.

But she was also fed up. She was twenty-nine and she didn't want to be a receptionist any more. Even in a trendy advertising office. She wanted to be creative. She wanted to do more than say: 'Hot Flash Advertising, can I help you?' a hundred times a day.

Her boyfriend, Dan, was torn. He wanted her to be happy but he knew she had no training for a creative job. And if she gave up her good job in Hot Flash, how could they afford the lovely luxury flat they were renting in Ringsend? That was why he never said anything when Clodagh got into one of her creative moods. In her last mood, she'd repainted the bathroom bright blue and made fish patterns in navy blue all along the bath. She had made a blind for the window all by herself. It looked beautiful, Dan admitted. But God knows what the landlord would say.

'Hot Flash Advertising, how can I help you?' said Clodagh wearily. It was nearly half five. She wanted to go home.

'Clodagh, it's me,' said Kim.

'Hello!' said Clodagh happily. She loved talking to her sister.

'Are you at home tonight?' asked Kim. 'I need to talk to you.'

'Yes,' said Clodagh. '*Coronation Street* is on the television tonight. Where else would I be?'

'I'll ring you after that,' said Kim. She said goodbye.

What was the big mystery? Clodagh wondered. She looked at the big silver clock on the wall. It was exactly half five. She put her special headset down and got up from her desk. If anyone wanted to phone now, tough bananas. They were too late.

★

That night, Kim and Clodagh spent half an hour on the phone.

'Poor Mum,' said Clodagh when she'd heard all the details.

'What do you mean *poor Mum*?' shouted Kim. 'It's me you should feel sorry for. These American girls are going to come and look down their noses at my house. They think I've got a housekeeper.'

Kim was getting more upset.

'Charleen's in college. She's very clever, Mother says. She probably has her own car at home. All American kids have their own cars. We can barely afford the van and my rust bucket. The house hasn't been touched in years. Tom painted the hall two years ago –

that's it. He did the girls' bedroom the year before. The living room is a mess and I hate that green colour in the bathroom. I can't have two strange girls move in and see the state of the place.'

'Calm down,' said Clodagh.

'I can't,' said Kim. She burst into tears. Her mother was ashamed of Kim and her family. That was it. Why else would she lie about Kim and her job? Why else would she lie about the big house and Tom's job? Because she was ashamed of Kim. That had to be the answer.

'She's not ashamed,' said Clodagh when Kim explained how she felt. 'Remember when I was ten or eleven. Miriam from across the road told me she was getting a bike for Christmas. I told her I was getting a bike *and* a dolls' house. I wasn't. I just didn't want her to think she was better than me. That's all.'

'Yes, but you were ten. Mother is an adult. She should know better,' said Kim sadly.

'Don't be silly, Kim. Of course Mum is proud of you. She has my head light every time I see her. "Why can't you be more like your sister?" she says. It's like listening to a broken record. Why can't you get married and settle down? She thinks that Dan and I are living a wild life and go to night clubs all week. She wants us to be like you and Tom.'

'Do you think so?' asked Kim. She wiped her eyes with a tissue.

'Yes.' Clodagh was cheerful. 'Don't panic. I have a plan. Let's all meet up in your house on Friday night. Tell Rob to come.' Rob was their older brother. He worked in the bank. He had four sons and was married to Jill. Jill was tall, blonde and thought she was the last word in style.

Elsie hated Jill. That was why she lived with Kim and not with Rob. Rob and Jill's house was bigger than Kim's. But if Elsie and Jill had to live together, even the UN wouldn't be able to keep the peace.

Clodagh wasn't fond of her sister-in-law either. Jill had once told Clodagh that she felt sorry for her for having red hair. Clodagh's hair was long, curly and the colour of flames. Clodagh had never forgiven Jill. Poor Rob was stuck in the middle. Family get-togethers could be deadly. At Christmas, Jill, Clodagh and Elsie had to be kept well apart from each other. After the argument last year about whether to watch *Titanic* or a ballet special, Kim had decided against having Christmas dinner in her house.

'I bet Mother didn't have to tell Aunt Maisie lies about Rob,' Kim said bitterly to Clodagh.

'Don't be silly,' Clodagh said. 'She probably said Jill was a nice person. That's a lie for a start.'

★

There were seven of them around the small dining room table. Clodagh had brought her boyfriend, Dan. Rob had brought a pot plant for his mother and a box of chocolates for Kim. He hadn't brought Jill.

Thank God for that, thought Elsie. Jill would look down her long nose at Elsie when she heard what had happened.

'What's the plan, Clodagh?' asked Tom McDonnell. He felt sorry for his mother-in-law. She'd been boasting a little bit. So what? Lots of people did it.

'Interior decoration,' said Clodagh proudly.

'What?' said Tom.

'We're going to do up the house,' Clodagh said simply.

'We can't afford an interior decorator,' Kim said, shocked. Those people charged a fortune to tell you what colour wallpaper to use. She'd seen them on the telly. They never used the cheapest wallpaper. Oh no. They went mad and did things with paint and bits of scarves draped over lamps.

'We're not hiring anyone,' Clodagh said. 'I'll do the designing and the rest of you will help out with the donkey work. All you need is clever ideas. You can do it really cheaply.'

'Like you did our bathroom,' said

Dan. Clodagh had primed him beforehand on what to say.

'Exactly,' said Clodagh. 'I've got some wonderful ideas. You've been saying for ages that it needs to be repainted, Kim. We'll all help and it will be beautiful. Then you won't mind Charleen and her friend staying. If they ask, you can say you got tired of the country and the horses. They won't ask,' she added confidently. 'Say you like living near the city because you are at the centre of everything. You have shops and cafés round the corner. You can hear the bells of Christ Church. You're minutes away from Stephen's Green. Tell them you wanted to be more cosmopolitan.'

'I thought that was a girls' magazine,' joked Dan.

Clodagh shot him a look. 'It means

that you wanted to live in the centre of a big, exciting city.'

'We'll say we're far too old for ponies,' Laura said. She loved this idea.

'We can say we wanted to be nearer the shops,' said Emer. That was true. Emer lived for the shops. Her side of the bedroom was like a sale of work with clothes everywhere.

'I've got great ideas for painting up the bathroom and the kitchen,' Clodagh said.

The rest of the family began to get excited too.

'I could put up those shelves in the sitting room,' said Tom. 'They're still in the box under the stairs. And I could make a special shelf for the television and video.'

'We could have window boxes,' said Elsie. She loved gardening. She had magic fingers with plants. But she hadn't bothered since her husband had died. This was Kim's garden and it would be rude to take over. Kim was bad with plants. She had only to look at an ivy and it dropped dead. 'We could re-do all your garden pots, Kim,' she said.

'Exactly,' said Clodagh. 'Dan can help with the garden.'

'I sell insurance,' said Dan nervously. 'I don't know how to garden.'

Clodagh tickled him under the chin. 'You know how to dig, don't you?' she said.

Rob said he had a load of paint in his loft. It was left over from the last time he'd had the house done. He knew where they could get nice patio slabs cheap and he had a friend who had a garden centre. They could get lots of plants at cost price.

Kim was the only one who was

quiet. 'We can't afford it,' she said. 'What's the point in painting the kitchen when the units are orange.'

'We can paint them too!' said Clodagh cheerily. 'I've seen them do it on the TV.'

'We'll all chip in, Mum,' said Emer.

'I'll buy the paint,' offered Rob.

'I'll buy patio slabs,' said Tom.

'I'll buy plants,' said Elsie.

'And we can do all the work ourselves,' Clodagh added.

'What about the housekeeper, and me being the school principal?' demanded Kim. 'I'm not lying to those two girls. I won't do it. It's wrong.' There was no way she was going to be involved in such a lie. Kim believed in telling the truth. She spent her life telling the children in school that the truth was important. It would be wrong of her to tell such huge lies. She wouldn't do it.

Tom decided it was time for his opinion. He'd been worried about how upset his wife was about the whole stupid thing. 'There'll be no lying in this house,' he said firmly. 'You *aren't* the principal, we *don't* have a housekeeper and there are *no* ponies.'

'They'd never fit in the garden,' joked Emer, looking into the tiny square of grass out the back.

Tom continued. 'Nobody is going to lie to Charleen and her friend. They can stay here and be welcome. That's all we're doing, making them welcome. The house could do with a lick of paint. And if the house looks nice, you'll feel better about the visitors, Kim. But if they ask, we'll tell them the truth. There's no housekeeper and there never was. Nobody will mention anything to do with ponies and you being the principal.'

'Ah come on, Mum,' said Emer. 'It'll be a bit of fun. You're always saying I spend too much time doing nothing in the summer holidays. It'll be cool to have Charleen here.'

Kim looked at the eager faces. 'As long as I don't have to spend my holidays working,' she said.

Chapter Four

Clodagh's project filled her mind all day. When she wasn't answering the phone in Hot Flash, she looked through magazines for ideas. She got gardening books from one of the women at work. She watched television programmes about gardens. Her favourite was one where TV gardener, Alan Titchmarsh, changed a garden totally in two days. The revamp was always a big secret. The owner was nearly always speechless when they saw how different it all looked.

Clodagh had dreams at night about what she would do to Kim's garden. She woke Dan up one night with her sleep-talking.

'Pink, pink, I want pink paint,' she muttered.

The next day, Dan teased her about it.

'Aren't you lucky,' she laughed. 'I could be shouting out another fella's name.'

'If you shout another fella's name, it'll be Alan Titchmarsh,' Dan said.

In the evenings, she sat at the coffee table and drew plans. She had different pages with colour schemes for each room. Dan said it all looked great.

'I don't know,' Clodagh said slowly. She stared at her plans. 'How hard is it to lay patio slabs?'

Dan hadn't a clue. 'Tom will know,' he said hopefully.

'Tom's an electrician,' Clodagh pointed out.

The plans for the inside of the house were more simple. Everyone knew how to paint. The twins had promised to help her with the special details.

She was going to paint sea creatures in the bathroom. Emer and Laura were going to paint the fish. Clodagh was going to do the seahorses herself because they were hard to do.

The living room was very dull so Clodagh planned to make it look lively. Bright sunshine colours would be great. And she had a plan to get plenty of big, bright pictures for free. Ones in shops cost a fortune but Clodagh knew a man who had art on the brain. He worked in a boring job and painted at the weekend. He'd be pleased to have his paintings hanging somewhere other than his mother's house.

Kim would have to make curtains, Clodagh decided. She had a sewing machine. Elsie could help her. Clodagh had already bought some of the material in a fabric sale. She'd bought yards of cheap muslin material in cream. It was for the windows. In one of her decorating books, it explained how to paint a pretty gold pattern onto muslin. She was dying to try it. Then, you draped the muslin on the window. It couldn't be too hard, could it?

But what she really couldn't wait to start was the dining room. Charleen and her friend were going to sleep there. Clodagh had it all worked out. She had her eye on a sofa bed that would look perfect with her colour scheme. Kim would probably be a bit shocked by the colour. Kim liked everything cream or white.

Clodagh was planning on a bold

russet colour. Clodagh decided to paint that room when Kim and the twins were in Brittas. That way, her sister wouldn't get upset at the sight of the paint in the tins.

★

Emer and Laura went into the big chemist in Stephen's Green to buy hair dye. There was an entire section full of the stuff. They stared at the shelves. 'How do you pick one?' asked Laura. She had never really looked at all the different hair colours before. She was amazed there were so many.

Emer was a bit surprised herself. On the television ads, they only showed a few colours. A blonde, a red and a dark brown, maybe. But here there were hundreds of boxes of colour.

There were white blondes, golden blondes and ash blondes. There were ones that you had to paint on, like highlights from the hairdresser. Laura picked up one with a picture of a woman with huge blue eyes and a golden mane of hair.

The sisters stared at the picture. The woman looked like she'd just stepped off a movie set. She looked stunning. She looked like Emer wanted to look.

'That's the one,' said Emer.

*

Dear Maisie,

We'd love to have Charleen and her friend to stay with us. We will be delighted to meet them at the airport. Kim's two daughters are lovely girls and very clever. They will show Charleen around if she would like. They have lots of trips lined up. Did I tell you that Emer got first place in her class in Irish recently?

Elsie paused in her letter writing. She was going to mention that Clodagh was going to give up her job to do a course in interior design. But she thought better of it. Clodagh had talked about giving up her job, but she hadn't. And Elsie had got into enough trouble stretching the truth. She didn't want to push her luck. She wrote:

Clodagh would love to give up her job to do a course in interior design. But it would be hard to give up such a good job. And the course is very expensive.

That sounded better.

*

On the third Thursday in June, Kim bought wine in the supermarket and picked up a big cream cake. She had steak, chicken and potatoes wrapped in tin foil all ready to go on the barbecue. Elsie helped her set up chairs and the picnic table in the garden.

Every time there was a noise on the street, Kim jumped. She was waiting to hear the twins come home.

'You're like a cat on a hot tin roof,' said Elsie when Kim jumped for the third time.

'It's a big day,' said Kim, 'the last exam. I hope they did all right.'

'No matter, don't mention the exam,' Elsie advised.

Tom arrived home at six.

'Where are the girls?' he asked.

Kim sighed. 'There's no sign of them,' she said. 'I don't know what could have happened. They said they'd be home by now ...'

The doorbell rang but it was only Clodagh and Dan.

'Where are the girls?' demanded Clodagh. She'd brought a big box of chocolates for them to celebrate the end of their exams.

'They're probably still with their friends, laughing their heads off because they're on their holidays,' Tom said.

Kim was still worried.

'I'm starving,' Dan said hopefully. He looked at the wine on the picnic table. 'I could kill for a drink.'

By half six, the barbecue was cooking away. Dan had drunk two glasses of wine. Clodagh had opened the chocolates and eaten four. She'd go on a diet tomorrow. She couldn't diet when there was barbecue food around. Elsie sat in the most comfortable deck chair and rested her feet.

Suddenly, they all heard the front door slam.

'Thank God,' said Kim.

Laura appeared, still in her school uniform. 'Sorry we're late,' she said. 'We went to Fiona's house.'

Her mother hugged her. 'I was worried about you. How did you get on?'

Laura looked a bit nervous. 'Oh, all right ...' she said.

'Have you left any food for me?' said a voice. It was Emer. Emer with bright blonde hair.

Everyone stared at her in shock.

'So that's why you were late,' said Clodagh.

'Emer!' said Kim.

'Look at your hair!' said Elsie.

Tom McDonnell looked at his daughter. She had left the house that morning with long dark hair. She'd be sixteen soon. She was growing up. 'I suppose you want the first baked potato because you've finished your exams?' he said.

Emer grinned. 'Yeah, Dad, that'd be cool.'

Laura sighed with relief. If Dad didn't mind the hair, everything was going to be all right.

'Why did you do that to your hair?' asked Elsie.

Emer patted her long blonde curls. 'I wanted to look nice for Charleen,' she said.

Chapter Five

On the first Saturday of the great decorating job, everyone wanted to use the wallpaper stripper.

Emer demanded the first go: 'I've seen them do this on the telly,' she said. 'It's easy.'

After ten minutes, she wanted to give it back. It was the hottest job ever. Steam rose from the stripper all the time. The person using the stripp-er was permanently covered in a cloud of steam.

'You asked for it,' said her father from the top of the ladder. He was slowly stripping wallpaper with a scraper.

'Think of it as a type of skin treatment,' Clodagh said. 'People pay good money to have their faces steamed.'

Emer was stuck with the steamer.

By six that night, they were all sick of it. But the walls in the sitting room were bare.

'Tomorrow, we'll do the hall,' said Clodagh. She was in charge of the plans.

'Can't we have tomorrow off?' begged Emer. Watching television shows about doing up houses and actually doing them up were very different.

'No,' said Clodagh. 'Dan and I are going to get us a takeaway from the chipper for a treat. Who wants what?'

★

It was a fantastic summer. As good as being in Spain, thought Kim, as she lay on the deck outside the mobile home on their last day away. She'd got a suntan and so had the twins. Even Elsie had freckles on her arms. The only person who was still pale was Clodagh.

'I'm as white as a milk bottle. I haven't had a chance to sit in the sun,' she told Kim the last time they spoke on the phone. Clodagh was spending every spare moment doing up the McDonnell house. In the two weeks that Kim and the girls had been away, she'd been finishing it.

'What have you done, exactly?' asked Kim. She was a bit nervous about the whole thing. When they'd gone away, there wasn't much painting done. Tom, Rob and Dan had laid a patio. Elsie had bustled about with plants. Kim hadn't seen her mother so happy in ages.

'You need a couple of geraniums there,' Elsie would say, looking at a patch of earth. 'And I love roses. A small bush would be nice. Bright pink is my favourite colour.'

Bright pink was Clodagh's favourite colour too. She couldn't wear pink, not with her red hair. So Kim was afraid that Clodagh would have gone mad and done the walls pink. Kim didn't think she could live with pink walls. What was wrong with cream wallpaper, anyway?

The following day, Kim parked the Mini outside the house in Dublin. Emer, Laura and Elsie got out. Clodagh's car, which was even more rusty than Kim's, was parked outside.

'I can't wait to see what Clodagh's done,' said Emer eagerly.

'Neither can I,' said her mother.

Kim opened the front door nervously and stepped into the hall. For a moment, she thought she was in the wrong place.

'Oh,' she said. Her hall table was still there and on it was the same old lamp she'd got as a wedding present. The coatstand was the same too. But the walls ... Kim stared around in wonder. The cream wallpaper with a pale pink stripe was gone. Now the walls were a rich green colour. Ivy was carefully hand-painted up the walls. The painted ivy trailed along over a mirror. Kim looked more closely at the mirror. It was her old one. But it had been covered with gold paint and made to look really old and expensive.

A huge real ivy sat on the hall table. There were photo frames beside it, full of pictures of the family. Clodagh had put them in gold, hand-painted frames.

Kim peeped into the living room. It had been a mushroom colour once. Now, it was bright cheery yellow with bits of blue here and there. It looked like a different room. Kim realised that her old cream curtains had been dyed a sunshine yellow. The armchairs and couch were covered with soft yellow throws. Fat bright blue cushions lay on the armchairs. Clodagh was lying on the couch.

'I'm exhausted,' Clodagh said. She had a cup of tea in one hand and she wore jeans with paint marks all over them. Clodagh's fingers were covered with paint too. Her red hair had wild yellow and green streaks in it.

'But I enjoyed it, you know,' Clodagh said.

Kim looked around in awe. The

room was like one from a magazine. Everything looked great because of Clodagh's bright new colours. She had turned a tired room into something special.

'It's like a different house,' Kim said.

'I know,' said Clodagh proudly. 'I think I'm good at this interior decoration stuff.'

'Good isn't the word,' said Kim. 'You're brilliant.'

Emer and Laura grinned. 'Wait till you see the bathroom, Mum,' said Laura.

They all trooped up to the bathroom. It was like diving into the sea. Clodagh had painted it in deep blues like the ocean. At the bottom, there were fishes and sea creatures like starfishes. The tiles had fishy designs on them too. Higher up, the walls were a paler blue, like the sea near the surface. There were pale blue towels and a pale blue blind. It must have all taken days to paint.

Kim hugged her sister tightly. 'You've worked so hard,' she said.

'Do you like it?' asked Clodagh.

Kim could barely speak. She wanted to cry instead. 'It's beautiful,' she said finally. 'Really beautiful.'

Chapter Six

Charleen and Pamela looked eagerly out of the plane window. Thousands of feet below them was Ireland. From the air, it looked like a pretty green patchwork quilt. It really was emerald, Charleen thought in surprise. Grandma was always talking about how green Ireland was. And how friendly the people were.

On St Patrick's Day, she would have a sip of sherry and get tears in her eyes. She would cry a bit. 'I'm sorry I never went home to Ireland,' she'd say sadly.

'Chicago is your home now,' Charleen's mom would say firmly. Charleen's mom, Sandra, had never wanted to visit Ireland. She preferred Florida. She liked the sun.

'I don't get much vacation time,' she said. 'And I don't want to spend it in the rain.'

'It rains in Chicago,' Grandma would argue. 'It snows too. It doesn't snow that much in Ireland.'

Charleen wished her mom and Grandma wouldn't argue so much.

As the plane landed at Dublin airport, Charleen began to feel really excited.

'We're in Europe!' she whispered to Pamela.

The two girls grinned happily at each other.

'I hope the McDonnells are nice people,' Charleen said. That was the only scary thing. She'd never met her Irish family. Now she'd be stuck with them for two weeks.

'They sounded nice in the letter your granny's sister sent,' said Pamela.

'Yes,' said Charleen nervously. Grandma had told her lots about her cousins. They sounded very different from the Chicago side of the family. Grandma said they were very clever girls and had been to France and everything.

★

Emer was wearing new jeans and high boots. She had put half a can of hairspray in her blonde hair to make it sit flat. Her make-up had taken an hour. It was very hot in the airport and her high heels were killing her. But she didn't care. She looked good. That was the most important thing.

Laura was wearing her old jeans and flip flops. If Emer was going to dress up to the nines, she would dress down. Whoever said that twins did everything the same was mad.

Elsie and Kim looked as if they were going out to a party. Elsie was in her Sunday best outfit and was carrying her good white handbag.

'Mother, sit down,' said Kim.

'It would be rude to sit down,' said Elsie. Despite the house being done up, she was still nervous.

'Mother, they're two eighteen-year-old girls,' said Kim crossly. She was nervous too. 'They could be ages getting their luggage. I wonder where Clodagh is?'

They needed two cars to bring everyone and the luggage from the airport. Clodagh said she'd come to give moral support.

She arrived just in time.

Two very ordinary looking girls in jeans came out of the arrivals door. They were pushing a big trolley. They looked around and saw the big sign that Emer had made.

'Welcome Charleen and Pamela,' it read in big writing.

'That must mean us,' said Pamela, seeing the sign.

The Dublin branch of the family smiled at the visitors.

'Hi,' said Charleen nervously. 'Are you the McDonnells?'

'Yes,' said Kim. 'Welcome, I'm your aunt Kim.'

She was pleased to see that both girls looked friendly and unsure. They weren't wearing lots of expensive clothes. They looked like ordinary teenagers.

Elsie was pleased to see that Charleen looked a little like Maisie.

Emer was pleased that the American girls looked very normal, not like movie stars at all.

Laura was pleased that they were wearing jeans. She didn't want to spend two weeks with people who wanted to dress up all the time. It was bad enough sharing with Emer. Emer put on make-up to answer the front door.

Why were they all standing around like dummies? Clodagh wondered. Somebody had to take action. 'Lovely to meet you!' she said and hugged Charleen. Then she hugged Pamela. 'I'm Clodagh. Which is which?'

There was nobody like Clodagh to break the ice, Laura thought.

Soon, they were all smiling and

hugging. It was as if they'd known each other for years.

There was a big discussion on which car everyone was to go in. Clodagh took charge again. 'Right,' she said. 'Emer and Charleen can go with me. We'll take half the bags. Pamela and Laura can go with Kim and Mum. Right?'

Charleen had never seen a car as old as Clodagh's before.

'Hey, this is cool,' said Charleen. 'A classic car.'

'Yeah, right,' said Clodagh as she crunched the gears. 'A classic car.' She opened the window to let some air in. 'It's got classic air conditioning too.'

'What's that?' asked Charleen politely.

'No air conditioning!' laughed Clodagh.

Emer giggled and so did Charleen.

Everyone relaxed. Everything was going to be fine.

At the house, Kim put the kettle on and the twins showed the visitors where they were going to sleep.

'This is normally the dining room but we fixed it up for you,' said Emer.

The visitors looked around at the warm red walls. They looked at the huge watercolour pictures that Clodagh had got for next to nothing from her friend.

They admired the floaty cream curtains and the sofa bed covered in the same cream material. Clodagh had even dyed sheets and pillowcases to go with the walls.

'I love this house,' said Charleen. It was so different from her home in Crystal Lake. Her Mom and Grandma liked pale colours. But this Irish house was really unusual. Artistic, that was the word for it. The dining room was like a painting and the bathroom was something else. Charleen hoped she'd get a chance to lie in the bath and light all the tiny vanilla candles that surrounded it. She could lie back and look up at the rich blue walls. It was supposed to look like the sea and it really did.

The kitchen made her think of the pretty pale buildings in Miami, Florida. Charleen decided she'd take a photo to show her mom and Grandma. They'd love the McDonnells' house.

'Do you like Italian food?' asked Emer.

'Sure,' said Charleen.

'Great. We're going to an Italian restaurant tonight to celebrate your visit.'

Charleen smiled with pleasure. Her Irish family were so nice. The way

Grandma had described them, she didn't think they'd be friendly. But they were so warm and kind.

The Italian restaurant was lively and good value. The family sat at one long table and everyone talked loudly. Clodagh told them all that she was going to do part-time interior decoration.

'She's so clever,' said Dan proudly.

Emer said she'd help out as long as she didn't have to use the wallpaper stripper.

'I'd love to do something like that,' said Char-leen. 'I don't know what I want to do in college.'

'I thought you were going to be a dentist like your mother,' said Elsie sharply.

'Mom's not a dentist,' said Charleen in surprise. 'She works with a dental surgeon but she's a nurse. She would have liked me to be a dentist but I flunked chemistry and biology.'

Elsie's eyes were like saucers.

'I was sure she was a dentist. Tell me, your uncle is a doctor, right?'

'He is a doctor but not a medical doctor,' Charleen said. 'He works in a laboratory.'

Elsie's eyes got even bigger. What had Maisie been telling her all these years? That Sandra was a dentist and Phil was a doctor. It hadn't been true at all. She was about to say something about all of this when Kim looked at her.

'Mother,' she said firmly, 'would you like garlic bread?'

Elsie looked back at Kim. She could tell what Kim was really saying: Let's forget all about doctors, dentists, school principals and big houses and posh estates.

Elsie could take a hint.

'I'm so hungry,' she said. 'I'd love garlic bread.'

★

That night, Kim sat at her dressing table and rubbed cream on her face.

'I thought Elsie's eyes were going to pop out of her head,' said Tom with a smile. 'She looked amazed when Charleen said her mother wasn't a dentist. It sounds like your Aunt Maisie was telling the odd fib too.'

Kim smiled as if she'd known all along. 'No harm was done,' she said.

Tom thought of all the hassle of redecorating the house. He thought of how upset both Kim and Elsie had been. He thought of Kim worrying herself sick about the visitors before they came. He smiled back at his wife. 'No harm was done,' he agreed. 'And aren't Charleen and Pamela lovely girls?'

'Lovely,' Kim said. 'It's a pleasure to have them here.'

*

It was a warm afternoon a week later. The four girls had gone off into town to shop. They were all excited about buying T-shirts like ones in a Madonna video. Elsie thought it was dreadful the way popstars were taking holy names now. What was the world coming to?

She finished weeding the flower bed under the window. The bed on the other side needed weeding too. That was the thing about weeds. Once you finished one side of the garden, the other side was full of weeds again. Her knees didn't hurt a bit any more because she had a weeding stool. She sat on the stool and used the weeder with the long handle. A bee buzzed by lazily. On the wall, a robin sat and looked at Elsie. She made a tweeting noise to the robin. He put his tiny head to one side and looked at her with his shiny black eyes. Elsie felt happy. She loved gardening. Tom had given her a bit of the garden shed to use for seedlings. She planned to grow bulbs in there in the winter.

★

Maisie sat in the den in the house in Crystal Lake, Chicago. She had her old photo album on her lap. Maisie had felt sad ever since Charleen's phone call from Dublin.

'I'm having a great time, Grandma,' Charleen had said happily. 'I love it here. Everyone's so nice to us. And Auntie Elsie is just like you, Grandma. She's really kind.'

Maisie opened the first page of the album. The pictures weren't anywhere

near as good as the modern pictures
that Phil took with his camera. With
that, you could have big photos or
small ones or any size you wanted. But
Maisie still loved the old ones best. She
stared at a hazy black and white shot of
herself and Elsie. She had been around
eighteen, so Elsie must have been
seventeen. They were posed in their
best dresses outside the farmhouse.
Behind them, their mother's rambling
rose climbed up the wall. Their father's
old sheep dog sat at Elsie's feet,
enjoying the sun. Maisie's dress had a
big full skirt and she had a flower
brooch on her collar. She could
remember that dress as if it was
yesterday. It had been a rich French
blue with a white collar. Elsie's had
been pale pink with a cream collar.

They looked so young and so happy.
Funny, she couldn't remember where

they were going all dressed up. Or who had taken the picture. Elsie would remember, she was sure. Elsie had the best memory.

They used to talk about the old times in their letters. Elsie would write, 'Do you remember the day we went to McNiffe's for the hay making? You said you were in love with young Billy McNiffe and he got all shy?'

And sure enough, Maisie would remember it. She could almost smell the hay and the fun they had when it was dinner-time. The woman of the house would come down the field with the dinner. Everyone would be mad with hunger. There would be hot, sweet tea, thick homemade bread and plenty of cold meat.

Everyone would sit and eat. They'd laugh and joke. Life was so simple then. Elsie didn't write about the old days anymore. Her letters had been sadder since Ted had died.

Maisie felt a pang of guilt. She should have gone back to Ireland for her brother-in-law's funeral. She should have been there for Elsie.

The tears started to fall down her face. She and Elsie had been so close. And now look at them. They wrote letters out of habit. They talked about houses and jobs and clever grandchildren. Not about the real things in life. They hadn't talked on the phone since last Christmas. That had to change, Maisie decided suddenly.

She got to her feet and went to the phone in the hall. She sat down at the small table and thought for the hundredth time that the hall furniture was getting tatty. It wasn't that she couldn't afford to replace it. Her late husband's insurance policy had left her well off. But she was nervous of spending the money. She'd never been used to spending. Now, she was worried about the kids. Sandra had always had trouble getting alimony out of her ex-husband. Phil never had a cent. He was hopeless with money, even thought he got well paid in the university. Maisie liked to think that when she died, her children and grandchildren would be well looked after.

But why not spend the money now? Why not visit her beloved sister in Ireland? Didn't they always say at home, 'There's no pockets in a shroud'. The kids would manage without every dollar of the insurance money. They never asked for it anyway. Maisie had a right to use her own money.

It took Maisie a while to find the number and a bit longer to dial it.

'Hello,' said a tired, old voice at the other end.

Maisie felt the tears behind her eyes again. When had her sister started sounding so old?

'Elsie, love,' she said hoarsely. 'It's me, Maisie. I don't suppose I could come for a visit?'

'Oh Maisie,' said Elsie. 'I thought you'd never ask.'money, even thought he got well paid in the university. Maisie liked to think that when she died, her children and grandchildren would be well looked after.

But why not spend the money now? Why not visit her beloved sister in Ireland? Didn't they always say at home, 'There's no pockets in a shroud'. The kids would manage without every dollar of the insurance money. They never asked for it anyway.

Maisie had a right to use her own money.

It took Maisie a while to find the number and a bit longer to dial it.

'Hello,' said a tired, old voice at the other end.

Maisie felt the tears behind her eyes again. When had her sister started sounding so old?

'Elsie, love,' she said hoarsely. 'It's me, Maisie. I don't suppose I could come for a visit?'

'Oh Maisie,' said Elsie. 'I thought you'd never ask.'

OPEN DOOR SERIES

Driving With Daisy by Tom Nestor

It All Adds Up by Margaret Neylon

Has Anyone Here Seen Larry?
by Deirdre Purcell

SERIES FOUR

Fair-Weather Friend by Patricia Scanlan

The Story of Joe Brown by Rose Doyle

The Smoking Room by Julie Parsons

World Cup Diary by Niall Quinn

The Quiz Master by Michael Scott

Stray Dog by Gareth O'Callaghan

ORDER DETAILS OVERLEAF

TRADE/CREDIT CARD ORDERS TO:
CMD, 55A Spruce Avenue,
Stillorgan Industrial Park,
Blackrock, Co. Dublin, Ireland.
Tel: (+353 1) 294 2560
Fax: (+353 1) 294 2564

TO PLACE PERSONAL/EDUCATIONAL
ORDERS OR TO ORDER A CATALOGUE
PLEASE CONTACT:
New Island, 2 Brookside, Dundrum
Road, Dundrum, Dublin 14, Ireland.
Tel: (+353 1) 298 6867/298 3411
Fax: (+353 1) 298 7912
www.newisland.ie